AF229284

Contents

Introduction

Sex window is a term you must have never come across but is essential part of everyone. Whether you are a kid/old man you have a window in your personality that you know little about and this is sex window.

The sex window

source:https://unsplash.co
m/search/photos/sexuality(
free photo)

what is sex? This is not an old question, but a question bubbled out of a new scheme of things in life. Sex is everywhere. It is in the office, house, street, market. Yes, sex is in the city, not just bedroom. It has come into lifestyle not be missed anywhere one can think of. It has become a point of view. sex can mean many things; can be many things to many people. sex in America may not be same as sex in India or South Africa. It appears it can't mean same thing. Geographies, life styles, circumstances, different people in different cultures and their sexual practices all make up the difference. what is sex in our lives today might turn into something not exactly sex tomorrow. sex may be fulfilling or not depends not just on bed partners but also surrounding situations, people in family, practices that fulfill bed mates; It all depends on the sex partners. Let's dig into sex a bit.

Everybody has a sex window. whether you are boy or girl, man or women it has no exception. only you have to be associated with sex. This means you need to be related to sex.one may be of any age, religion or belief.one can't deny presence of this window because it is part and parcel of person yet invisible and hidden. next most important question is does it have any physical basis? yes it has. just the way love can have a physical basis this sex window too has a physical basis. If one argues that love has no reality or relation in life then sex window may be an equal argument for such a person. This thing, of course, may not hold true as it has to be as impressive as love from point of view of medical Science. As any person is born feeling of love open up and as baby grows and faces different situations in life love is shaped as part of mind/body. a sex window may be thought of as neglected and unnoticed in case of children. But, as baby becomes boy/girl and boy/girl enters puberty physical changes take place and (sex)window opens. this happens in majority of cases and from then, sex window associates with the person's life. It(sex window)lasts till death.

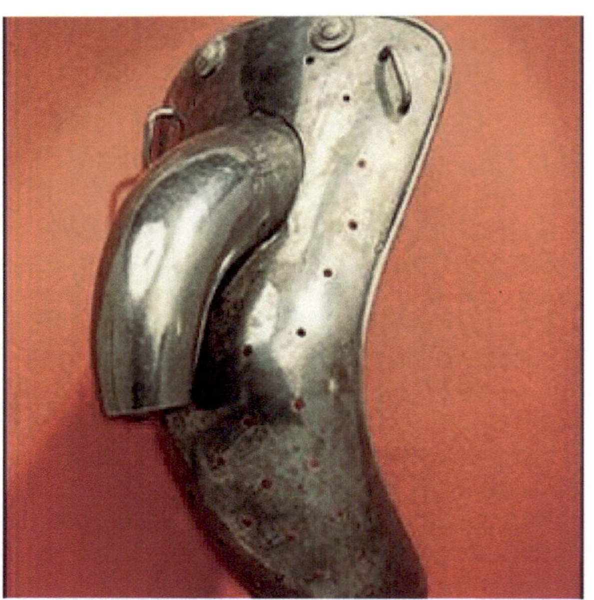

Male anti-masturbation device, 1880-1920. © Science Museum, London

Once upon a time, there used to be era of romance and love. moralism and scientific investigation produced ideas of orthodox human sexuality based on a combination of social and biological ideas. Popularly expressed, this amounted to 'Hogamus higamus'. What men are habitually, women are only exceptionally so. In Victorian age [1837-1901] this used to be situation where girls are engulfed with feelings of shy, downcast looks which gave way in time to naughty, coy upright girls image. what happens to sex window in case of lovers? what happens to it in case of Strangers? These are the questions that come to people introduced to this new (sex)window in 21st century.

Theoretically, sex window begins to show changes in Lovers. In a stark sex activity sex window is opened wide and as desires are fulfilled and bed-mates return to their rest state, sex window too returns to its normal size. In case of Strangers sex window is passive, unresponsive in such a manner that sex windows of 2 strangers (people) doesn't match and so inactive. This occurs only if they are strangers in physical true sense.

<u>sex fiction</u>

<u>Source:</u> sex and city
wallpapers

fictitious writing involving sex window or its experiences is sex fiction. what is non-fiction then? first, erotic fiction or fantasy may be offshoot of authors who use their experience/knowledge of their sex window. fantasy is far from reality and it is imagination which is limited only by mind of fantasy writers. ghost writers too may make good money with this new sex fiction. If sex window is a reality, isn't sex fiction too a reality!?yes and no. not all sex fiction writings are real. line of demarcation between non-fiction and fiction becomes thinner and thinner. With sex window writing personal experiences may come up in black and white on paper(i.e in a book).

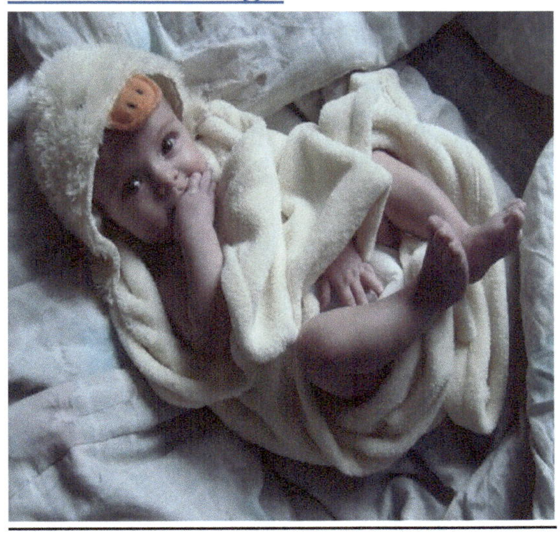

Source:https://www.freeim
ages.com/photo/baby-
1434491(free image)

sex window for a toddler is almost non-existent. As a baby grows in age becomes a boy and matures into puberty sex window naturally opens. A male sex window is same as female sex window only in concept yet it is not so factually. Are all desires of man same as desires of woman? no, emphatically. Similarly, man's sex window is not same as women's sex window. Furthermore, man is not directly in control of man's sex window. same is the case for the women. The only way in which one can assert a sex window is through action of sex. A sex window of old person is similar to that of a child in general.

courtesy:
Commons.wikimedia.org
courtesy: *The Sulaimaniya
Museum, Iraq.*

Photo © Osama S.M Amin

mating of 2 persons of opposite sex with similar sex window may be termed as sex window adventure. Certainly, that mating might be satisfactory and personally invigorating to their temper for the 2 persons. a sex orgy party may allow people with similar sex windows and they may eventually have deep realization. This may happen or in most cases not happen as these sex window adventures are guided tours whose end result depends on initiating practitioner. This is certainly, not a one-night stand in general. personal realization through sex is a debatable and controversial topic in itself. It has to be mentioned that sex window adventures may also stem from imagination which is not a normal and common possibility in all cases. Every straight sex person is entitled to a sex window adventure by virtue of birth itself.

Courtesy:www.freeimages.
com

Not all sexes are same. male and female; man and woman are not the only genders existing in the world. we have a third sex of gay/lesbian. Gays/lesbians too have a sex window but their sex window is not normal. It is not straight which does not mean that they have to see a doctor (sexologist like). a sex window once broken can't be bought to same condition as it was before.

sex window can be corrected to some extant if not fully because every person is born with a sex window and dies with one. sex window practitioners of tomorrow may know intimately about their patients and are responsible for happy living of their wards.

CREDIT: COURTESY OF UNIVERSAL

All sexually active in life,
Men/women and boys/girls
are freed from agony of
their personality windows

taking away their precious freedom. This is the age of unearthing one's sex window and finding matching mate suitable and able both in bed and at home. Have a happy sexual living.

www.ingramcontent.com/pod-product-compliance
Lightning Source LLC
Chambersburg PA
CBHW041233050726
47599CB00007B/939